SOFIA MARTINEZ

The Secret Recipe

by Jacqueline Jules

illustrated by Kim Smith

PICTURE WINDOW BOOKS
a capstone imprint

Sofia Martinez is published by
Picture Window Books, a Capstone imprint
1710 Roe Crest Drive
North Mankato, MN 56003
www.mycapstone.com

Library of Congress Cataloging-in-Publication Data
Jules, Jacqueline, 1956- author.
The secret recipe / by Jacqueline Jules ; illustrated by
Kim Smith.
pages cm. -- (Sofia Martinez)

Summary: Sofia helps her grandmother make her
special rice pudding, but there is a mix-up in the
recipe.

ISBN 978-1-4795-8717-9 (library binding)
ISBN 978-1-4795-8723-0 (pbk.)
ISBN 978-1-4795-8727-8 (ebook pdf)

1. Rice puddings--Juvenile fiction. 2. Cooking--
Juvenile fiction. 3. Grandmothers--Juvenile fiction.
4. Hispanic Americans--Juvenile fiction. 5.
Grandmothers--Fiction. [1. Cooking--Fiction.
2. Grandmothers--Fiction. 3. Hispanic Americans--
Fiction.] I. Smith, Kim, 1986- illustrator. II. Title.
III. Series: Jules, Jacqueline, 1956- Sofia Martinez.

PZ7.J92947Se 2016
[E]--dc23   2015024977

Designer: Kay Fraser

Printed in the United States of America in
North Mankato, Minnesota.
092015 009221CGS16

TABLE OF CONTENTS

CHAPTER 1

Cooking with Abuela

On Saturday afternoon, Sofia rushed over to Abuela's house. Abuela was making arroz con leche for the church supper.

Sofia loved helping her abuela cook, and her abuela loved spending time with Sofia.

Abuela stirred the rice in a giant pot. Sofia went to the pantry to get the sugar.

"¡Cuidado!" Abuela called. "Be sure to get the container with the red lid, not the green one."

Just then, the doorbell rang.

It was the next door neighbor,

Mrs. Flores.

"The special ingredient for your

arroz con leche," Mrs. Flores said,

handing over a small bag.

Sofia snuck around the corner to listen. She was curious. What did Abuela put in her rice pudding that made it so special?

"Gracias," Abuela said. "I am glad you had some. I did not want to go shopping again."

Sofia quickly got bored and hurried back to the kitchen. She grabbed a container filled with white crystals.

She was not paying attention. Her mind was still on that little blue bag.

Sofia did not notice that she took the container with the green lid, not the red one.

"Add three cups of sugar to the pot," Abuela called. She was still talking to Mrs. Flores.

Sofia carefully measured three cups. She poured them into the pot and kept stirring.

Then Sofia put the container with the white crystals back in the pantry and cleaned up.

She was proud that Abuela trusted her to help.

"¡Muy bien!" Sofia said when they were finished cooking.

"Would you like to take a little home for tomorrow's breakfast?" Abuela asked.

"Definitely!" Sofia said.

CHAPTER 2

The Mistake

The next morning, Sofia had breakfast with Mamá. They shared the arroz con leche.

Sofia took a bite first. She made a face and spit it out.

"¿Qué pasa?" Mamá asked.

"Salty!" Sofia ran to the sink with a glass. "¡Agua!"

Sofia remembered going into the pantry the day before. Abuela had warned her to get the jar with the red lid, not the green one. She had picked the wrong one!

"Oh, no! We need to make more pudding," Sofia said. "This time with sugar instead of salt."

"Sí," Mamá said. "I should have everything we need."

Mamá put rice, cinnamon sticks, milk, vanilla, and sugar on the kitchen counter.

"It smells like you're making rice pudding," Papá said. He had just walked into the kitchen with Sofia's sisters.

"Only Abuela makes arroz con leche," Luisa said.

"Yo sé," Sofia explained. "This is an emergency."

Soon, the whole family was busy cooking.

Just as they were finishing,

Sofia remembered something.

"We don't have the special

ingredient!" she yelled.

Sofia told her family about the

bag Mrs. Flores had brought over.

"Un misterio," Mamá said.

"I'm not sure what it was."

"Will the arroz con leche still taste good?" Sofia asked.

"I hope so," Papá said.

"Me too," said Sofia quietly.

"Me too."

CHAPTER 3

The Big Switch

Mamá put the arroz con leche into a serving pan to take to the church supper.

"We still have a problem," Luisa said. "Abuela will bring her pudding, too."

"That is problem," Mamá said.

"We have to take her pan off the table and put ours in its place," Elena said.

"No hay problema," Sofia said. "I'll keep her busy while Mamá makes the switch."

That night at the church, Sofia was nervous. As soon as she saw her abuela, Sofia ran toward her.

She pulled her grandmother's arm. "Will you come to the bathroom with me?" Sofia asked.

"¿Por qué?" Abuela asked.
"You don't need an old lady to
come to the bathroom with you."

"Por favor," Sofia pleaded.

Abuela was suspicious. "What's
going on?"

"Nada," Sofia said, trying to look innocent.

As Abuela turned around, she saw Mamá moving her arroz con leche off of the dessert table.

"Where are you going with my arroz con leche?" Abuela asked.

Sofia explained her mistake and how her family tried to help her fix it.

"I feel awful," Sofia said.

Abuela laughed. "You wanted to protect my feelings!"

"¡Claro!" Sofia said. "I love you!"

"Te amo mucho," Abuela said. "That's why I didn't say anything about your mistake. I didn't want to hurt your feelings."

"You knew?" Sofia asked.

"I had some for breakfast," Abuela said, smiling. "I made another pan after my first bite."

"I'm sorry I ruined our first pan," Sofia said. "I should have been more careful."

"It's okay, my dear," Abuela said. "It happens."

"Now we have two pans of pudding," Mamá said.

"But they are not the same," Sofia said. "Abuela has a secret ingredient in hers."

"What is this secret ingredient?"
Mamá asked.

"Lemon peel," Abuela said.

"And love," Sofia added. "Lots
and lots of love."

Spanish Glossary

abuela — grandmother

agua — water

arroz con leche — rice pudding

claro — of course

cuidado — careful

gracias — thank you

mamá — mom

muy bien — very good

nada — nothing

no hay problema — no problem

papá — dad

por favor — please

por qué — why

qué pasa — what's wrong

sí — yes

te amo mucho — I love you so much

un misterio — a mystery

yo sé — I know

Talk It Out

1. Do you like to help in the kitchen? Why or why not?

2. Do you think Sofia should have just told her Grandma what she did, or do you agree with her solution? Explain your answer.

3. How do you think Sofia felt when she realized she used salt instead of sugar?

Write It Down

1. How do you think Sofia's grandma reacted when she tasted the *arroz con leche?* Write about her reaction.

2. Make a grocery list of the ingredients you would need to buy to make your favorite recipe.

3. Write about a time when you made a mistake. Be sure to include how you felt when you realized it.

About the Author

Jacqueline Jules is the award-winning author of twenty-five children's books, including *No English* (2012 Forward National Literature Award), *Zapato Power: Freddie Ramos Takes Off* (2010 CYBILS Literary Award, Maryland Blue Crab Young Reader Honor Award, and ALSC Great Early Elementary Reads), and *Freddie Ramos Makes a Splash* (named on 2013 List of Best Children's Books of the Year by Bank Street College Committee).

When not reading, writing, or teaching, Jacqueline enjoys time with her family in northern Virginia.

About the Illustrator

Kim Smith has worked in magazines, advertising, animation, and children's gaming. She studied illustration at the Alberta College of Art and Design in Calgary, Alberta, where she now resides.

Kim is the illustrator of the middle-grade mystery series *The Ghost and Max Monroe*, the picture book *Over the River and Through the Woods*, and the cover of the middle-grade novel *How to Make a Million*.

FUN
doesn't stop here!

- Videos & Contests
- Games & Puzzles
- Friends & Favorites
- Authors & Illustrators

Discover more at
www.capstonekids.com

See you soon!
¡Nos Vemos pronto!